Gwillimbury Tales

© Heidi Klose 2017

Gwillimbury
Tales

© 2017 by Heidi Klose

Illustrations by Sylvia Somerville

Front and back cover photos courtesy of S. Somerville

Seagull Publications, Niagara Falls, Ontario

ISBN: 978-1-988031-07-1

Dedicated to my niece, Ramona, who has a wonderful smile, and an infectious laugh. She is someone who lights up a room, and makes everyone in it cheerful and happy to be there.

and to

Sylvia Somerville, who created the amazing illustrations of J.J., Serge, Milford and Porter. She also contributed her own photos of 'Gwillimbury Forest', which are actually of Sherwood Forest, for the front and back cover. Thank you, Sylvia, for all your help in making my manuscript into a marvelous book.

Prologue

This is a work of fiction. Names, characters, places and incidents either are the product of the author's imagination or are used fictitiously, and any resemblance to any actual persons, living or dead, events, or locales is entirely coincidental.

Working on this little book has also given me a lot of pleasure. I am very much impressed by a famous, I mean very famous, Canadian author, who, from time to time, writes children's literature. She likes to use a lot of alliteration. I thought I'd give it a go and mimic her style. In this book, I actually began with the third chapter about Milford the Mailman. Well, I had some success alliterating, but couldn't really do it throughout the whole book.

Why Gwillimbury? Well, my husband and I have a cottage on the French River. Every time we drive up the 400 Highway, a little south of Barrie and south-west of Orillia, we see a sign that says West Gwillimbury. I love the word 'Gwillimbury'. It dances around in my head. Reminds me of a lot of Welsh names that do the same thing, 'Gwendolyn', 'Gwyneth', 'Llewellyn'. They flow, just like 'lullaby'.

I once asked my daughter, Marnie, if there was an East Gwillimbury, and she said yes. I now know this to be true, because this past summer she and her teammates became the East Gwillimbury Ladies B League Soccer Champions! Well done, ladies. Now Marnie doesn't actually live in East Gwillimbury, but a little south-west of the town, in Aurora.

I could never write a book about Aurora, because I can't even form the word in my mouth. If someone I know, let's say Rory, actually lived on a Rural Route in Aurora, I would break off all forms of communication with him, because if someone were to ask me where he lived, there would be some garbled gurgling sounds gushing out of my mouth, trying to explain where. Very embarrassing! Thankfully Rory lives in Hamilton. I wonder if he has a middle name.

I would also like to say, that this little exercise in alliteration is by no means a social commentary on anyone in either East or West, or the imaginary North or South Gwillimbury. I am not Stephen Leacock, and this is not 'Mariposa' (Orillia). I have written this so that people who read it will smile a little, perhaps even laugh out loud. After all, in these very stressful times we all need to have a little humour to get us through each day.

Enjoy reading,

Heidi

To order: *heidi.klose@gmail.com*

CONTENTS

J.J. the Junior Reporter   Page   7

Serge, the Apprentice Electrician   Page   19

Milford the Mailman   Page   27

Porter the Pipefitter   Page   33

South Gwillimbury

J.J. the Junior Reporter

There is a town called South Gwillimbury. It is situated south-west of East Gwillimbury, south-east of West Gwillimbury and directly south of North Gwillimbury.

The town is a haven for seniors. Many citizens of East, West and especially North Gwillimbury have moved here in their retirement years because although it is only 5 km south of North Gwillimbury, the feeling is that summers are much longer and warmer here and winters are more bearable. North Gwillimbury brings images of eternal snow, mukluks and sled dogs, whereas images of South Gwillimbury are of palm trees, piña coladas and evening strolls on a sandy beach.

There are many senior homes in this town, one of these being *Tropical Breezes*. Tenants have their own apartments, but there are lounges where they, well, lounge. In one of these sitting rooms you will always see the same four people seated at the same table. They will sit and chat, read the local paper, or play hours of euchre.

One of these seasoned veterans is Gladys Illuminata. Before retirement she was a home economics teacher. Of course that was a very long time ago – before they discontinued home economics and shop classes at all the schools, and once that happened, Gladys was declared redundant. Well, her job was, and so for the last fifteen years of her teaching career she taught history.

At the same table sits Bernie Forthright, who had been in the military. Norman Digger was the third member of this group. He had been a Classics professor at the local university. Rounding out this happy quartet is Selma Parley, who had a long and tiring career working in Human Resources at the same local university.

All four read the local daily newspaper from beginning to end, because they had a lot of time. Given the fact that many people, especially the younger generation, no longer bought newspapers, because they received their news from the internet, from blogs and twittering and lord knows in what other manner of communication, and that advertising dollars were down, the local daily became the local weekly. This did not go well with Jack Brumble, the editor-in-chief of the *South*

Gwillimbury Gazette. He found it increasingly hard to keep his reporters because he could pay them so very little.

Another of his reporters had quit and moved on to the big city to further his career. Jack needed someone to write a column about local events and so he advertised the position but had one lowly applicant, J.J., who just happened to be his nephew.

"See here J.J.," said Jack, "I need someone to go to all the local events in our town and write an interesting column about it. Also, don't make it too long. Try to get as much information as possible into as tiny space as possible. We're printing less and less pages and I need to keep some room for the advertisements."

J.J. got right to it and went to a couple of bars where some local bands were playing. He enjoyed his outings, found the bands quite entertaining and promising, thought he would also comment on the food and beverages being served and wrote his column.

Jack, busy with his problems at the paper, neglected to read J.J.'s first literary novelty and so the article was published un-proofed. When Jack saw the article on page five of his paper he just about blew his top. He summoned his nephew and began to blast him. "What kind of chicken scratch is this?" he shouted.

"Well, Uncle Jack …," J.J. tried to explain.

"I've had all kinds of complaints from my readers. People can't figure out this gibberish and gobbledygook."

"Well, Uncle …," J.J. tried once more.

"It looks like you threw a bunch of letters together and didn't care where they ended up on the page. Is this some kind of a joke?" queried the editor-in-chief.

"No, sir, actually …," stumbled J.J.

"It's garbage, you're fired, you hear me?" responded Jack.

"Yes sir, quite well, but …," answered J.J.

"No buts. Butt out! Get out of my office. Get out, get out!" shouted Jack. "I have never been so embarrassed in my whole life. Try to do a favour for a family member and look what happens."

Poor J.J. never got to explain just what it was that he was trying to say in his column. With his head down, and quite dejected, he walked out of the building.

Back at *Tropical Breezes* four old friends were reading the *South Gwillimbury Gazette*. Each had tried to decipher the article that J.J. had written.

Bernie was the first to speak. "I have seen something like this before. This article is written in code. You know that I worked for counter intelligence during the Cold War. I am going back to my room to see if I can decipher this."

The others agreed that it would take some time to make headway with this article and so they each took their newspaper and the retirees retired to their apartments. Early the next morning they met for breakfast. Bernie spoke first, "I have made some progress. I believe that this is written in code and that the message is that we are going to be attacked by the Soviet Union very soon."

"That is ridiculous," countered Gladys. "The Soviet Union fell with the Berlin Wall back in 1989."

"That's right," responded Bernie, "but it is being resurrected. Why look at all the money they make from oil and natural gas. They want to be strong again and take over the world."

"That is pure and simple hogwash," retorted Gladys. "This isn't a military code at all. I have figured out exactly what it is. It's a pizza recipe. Here try a piece. I tried it out last night. What a scrumptious recipe – you simply use all the ingredients you have in your fridge. Very cheap and economical! This is something I could have taught my students way back when."

"Nonsense," replied Norman. "This is absolutely rubbish. I agree with Bernie that it is some kind of a cryptogram, but is has nothing to do with espionage. It is an ancient script used by aliens trying to communicate with us."

"Ridiculous," shouted Bernie

"Ludicrous", added Gladys.

"Quiet, all of you," shouted Selma, who had had a long history of diffusing difficult and explosive situations at the negotiating table. As a member of Human Resources she had worked hard bargaining for the administration with three different unions on campus. "Let Norman finish what he wants to say," she shouted. "You've all had your say, now it's his turn."

Norman continued. "You know that I've had a fascination with the possibility of alien contact. That's why I have learned many ancient languages such as Sanskrit and Quipa. There are signs of this in South America, signs of alien contact visible from the air. I knew that they would come back. This is their way of communicating with us and perhaps I am the only person who can figure it out. Think of the publications I could have. Think of the fame!" he sighed.

"Personally I think you're crazy," countered Gladys. "And I have read some of your articles, so I know this to be a fact."

"Oh hush up," yelled Bernie.

"Enough," shouted Selma.

J.J. to his astonishment was called back into the editor's office. "Young man, said the editor-in-chief, "young man, I must say that I am very surprised, to say the least, and amused. Your chicken scratches have found an audience. Why I've had so many compliments from my readers that I have decided to keep you on at the paper. I want you to continue *writing*, well that is certainly stretching it, for our newspaper.

At the seniors' home Gladys kept trying out new recipes, Norman tried to contact aliens and Bernie convinced his old pals from his working days to help in decoding the neo-Soviet messages, hoping to avert a take-over of North America.

One day his grandson came to visit him. Proudly Bernie showed him the articles and his interpretations.

This was one of the articles which his grandson read:

"DFs,

A B& iz playing @ a local bar, d lEd ;-o iz a real QT bt d bozo nhnd d keyboard shd kip his dy job. Aftr sum ≤) 2 mor imgoin 2 review noths nu b&"

"But granddad," said Bernie the younger, "those are not secret messages, those are just net lingo, acronyms. All it says is that a band is playing at a local bar, that the lead singer is a real cutie but that the idiot behind the keyboard should keep his day job. And, after some pizza tomorrow he is going to review another new band. All young people use this code to text their friends."

"Poppycock" replied Norman. "I know what it says, and that's that."

And so the younger South Gwillimates started to read the newspaper to get interesting information about what was happening around town from J.J.'s articles. All the older South Gwillimates interpreted these articles using their own experiences and imaginations. Some brought out their Ouija boards and used the secret language to communicate with their dearly departed. A research scientist was convinced that he had stumbled upon a code which could be a cure for some exotic disease. A physicist at the same university thought this was a new theorem that explained the origin of the universe. And at the local hairdresser's they thought that this was town gossip and so they tried to figure out who was having an affair with whom.

The only people who protested, at first, were teachers, because they thought that these were cheat notes for their tests, but since most of their pupils were still getting low grades, they reasoned that this wasn't possible.

Jack Brumble soon retired and J.J. became editor-in-chief of the local newspaper which again became a daily paper. **And ...**

West Gwillimbury

Serge, the Apprentice Electrician

There is a little town called West Gwillimbury. It is situated north-west of South Gwillimbury, south-west of North Gwillimbury and directly west of East Gwillimbury.

The folks of the town are a friendly sort and full of life. If you venture there you might view them in the great outdoors engaging in activities such as baseball, broomball, badminton, basketball, bowling on lawns and even throwing boomerangs. But wait! You are thinking that the participants of these activities are the children of the townspeople and that their parents are standing on the sidelines cheering them on.

No, no, there are only rare sightings of the children. You may get a glimpse of them sauntering onto a yellow banana bus taking them to school, but other than that, you won't see them scurrying about in the schoolyard at recess or lunch hour. No, they are safely hidden inside the school building, on the school bus and, right after school, at home in their bedrooms.

Yes, the junior West Gwillimates race to their bedrooms turn on their computers and try to connect with their peers and classmates. After all, they haven't seen each other in at least twenty minutes. They will chat in their chat rooms. They will post things on their Facebook. They will twitter and text on their cell phones and they will do this non-stop, with a little break to grab a snack and then go back into their bedrooms. Yes, they are addicted to electronic connectivity, enchanted with energy guzzling gadgets, hooked on hardware and slaves to software.

One day, one of these junior electronically linked West Gwillimates was having a conundrum with his computer. The screen had a scintillating shimmer, became bright as an exploding supernova, whimpered, imploded and went black. The puerile little person at first sat there with a blank face, which mirrored the computer monitor. He was dismayed that he had been disconnected from his universe. After about fifteen minutes of shock and disbelief that this could actually happen, he catapulted down the stairs and did the only thing he knew to do, he complained to his mother. She, the protector and guardian of all things that might in some shape or form bring distress to her child, who at first realized the benefit of some non-connectivity, saw the terror in her offspring's face. Her heart melted and she phoned the local electrician. To her dismay, the phone number no longer existed and she vaguely remembered that the business had been shut down because of the poor economic times and relocated in a larger city. She then recalled that her neighbour's son, Serge, had been an apprentice in this company.

She scurried to her neighbour's house and pleaded with Serge. "Please," she whined, "I envision that there is an error with the electrical connection to our emporium. There must have been a sudden surge, the computer glowed and then imploded. Please come and evaluate and explain to us our electrical non-connectivity." Serge, who was only early on in his apprenticeship as an electrician, had never been empowered or equipped to elicit confidence or know-how to fix a surge.

He entered the neighbour's house even so and embarked upon the evaluation of the electrical wires. "The explanation is right here," he said quite quickly. "Your wires have been extending beyond their limits and have been exposed to the elements for too long. It looks like your wires coming to the house have been rubbing against the branches of your evergreen trees and I think that some have worn through. I don't have the expertise or equipment to fix them, so please call someone from the city.

"No, no", erupted Mrs. Ellenvale, "that would take too long. Why I have heard that it might take a whole day before they come to our town. I can't wait that long. I am imploring, empowering and employing you to eradicate this situation. You will have to fix it today."

Serge protested vehemently, but he felt sorry for Mrs. Ellenvale and her son and so he began to repair the electrical wires. What ensued, he is not sure of, because he is still recovering in hospital with minor burns to his hands, and is just now coming out of his coma.

The wires he tried to reconnect blew a transformer on Mrs. Ellenvale's street. There was a chain reaction. I have forgotten to mention that it was a very hot and humid summer day and all the air conditioners were running at full capacity. Once the first transformer blew, all the transformers in the whole town followed and everything electrical went dead. It didn't just stop in

West Gwillimbury, you see, North, East and South Gwillimbury were on the same grid, and so once the West Gwillimbury transformers blew, all the others on the whole grid blew as well. There was silence.

There were no televisions telecommunicating, no computers connected, no cell phones calling. There was no texting or twittering or talking or blogging. There was nothing. Silence altered everything.

From the houses appeared pale and pallid little Gwillimates, rubbing their eyes as they had not encountered sunshine in ever so long a time. They stood as if transfixed in their front yards not knowing what to do.

Their parents, being more practical, thought of other things. "The food in our freezers and fridges is going to spoil if we don't do something quickly," they figured. They came up with a grand idea. They organized street festivals and block parties. They closed the streets to traffic and began hauling out their bbq's, placing them smack dab into the centre of the streets.

Everyone brought their perishable foods and soon you could smell hamburgers, steaks and hot dogs being prepared on the grills. Neighbours brought salads, cakes or other deserts, especially ice cream which has the habit of melting quickly in a non-electrified freezer. Soon there were grand street parties in every corner of North, South, East and West Gwillimbury. Neighbours were speaking with neighbours they hadn't seen in eons. They re-acquainted with old friends, made new ones and had a wonderful time.

And the children, well, with some guidance from their parents, brought out hockey nets and began to play road hockey, a very addictive, but healthy game. Soon boys and girls were deaking and swerving and running and shooting small balls; having the best time of their lives. And, they got to see their friends face to face without *Facebook*. "What a novel idea," they thought. This went on the entire summer.

Serge recovered completely from his shock and was released from the city hospital. The Gwillimates from all four directions collected an enormous amount of money and out of gratitude, and fear for their safety, gave Serge a huge scholarship to continue and finish his apprenticeship as an electrician. Once finished, they reasoned, he would come back to town and work in confidence, both his and theirs, to be the towns' electrician and serve them well.

Eventually power was restored and the children went back to their computers and cell phones, but those summer nights on the streets had made an impression and impact on them. They limited their electronic connectivity and began to enrol in hockey, indoor soccer, swimming and many other activities. Instead of texting, they bumped into their friends, quite literally, as one does in hockey, instead of twittering they tripped their playmates on the soccer pitch, which can be a tad painful, but a lot of fun. Instead of blogging they spoke with their friends face to face. The whole town had been transformed by exploding transformers, and saved by a surge, **and they ...**

North Gwillimbury

Milford the Mailman

There is a town called North Gwillimbury. It is situated north-west of East Gwillimbury, north-east of West Gwillimbury and directly north of South Gwillimbury.

In this small town people always like to complain. For example, last week Mrs. Bilberry belittled the baker. "His bread and buns always used to be made of better batter. Even his cookies and cakes that used to taste sweet as bonbons are now bitter," she babbled.

The week before that Mr. Mandrake critized the mechanic. "My magnificent motor machine has absolutely no movement. It stutters and stammers," he muttered.

Others had complained about the ghastly garbanzo beans of the green grocer; what a clumsy and crude craftsman the carpenter was; how the decorator's desire to deliver delightful decor had been disastrous; how the wine maker must have used wastewater for his wine because it tasted like vinegar.

Even the teacher was not spared. The town's brats were a blemish and blight to the borough and so the burden had to be put on to the educator for this big blunder.

Criticizing others seemed to be a competition among the citizens. Protesting on a podium in their little public park with painfully piercing public speaking was paramount.

There would soon be prominent need for public oratory. Things were about to progress or get poorer, but this is based upon your individual point of view.

Milford was a mild sort of nondescript man. He had managed a meager and mediocre means of livelihood in a minor mill which, given the mean economic times, had shut down. He made enquiries for other work and managed to become the local mail carrier. He was actually the single and solitary applicant for this position. Nobody else wanted to deliver soaked or saturated letters or packages, because of drizzle, downpour or driving rain. Therefore mild and meek Milford had not been tested as to whether he actually qualified to deliver periodicals and other publications to people.

So Milford began his great career as a mail person. It could have been stated here that he was a mailman, because he actually was a man delivering mail.

However, to say this is politically incorrect. Milford whistled a tune as he walked along and then very soon even began to sing a song. He felt that he had made it to the pinnacle of his pursuits. He was a bit bewildered by barking dogs, but they basically couldn't be bothered to bite him, only a bit.

Milford delivered a package to Mr. Nettle who in his nervous excitement naturally assumed, and had no doubt, that it belonged to him, extracted the contents immediately. Nevertheless, he was stunned and surprised to survey its contents and see that it was filled with CD's of rap music. Only then did he look at the addressee and perceive that the package was meant for the teenage progeny of his neighbour.

Mr. Fennel was flabbergasted to receive final notification that he was the front-runner in a friendly fiddling contest because, as everyone knew, he couldn't carry a tune.

Mrs. Culpepper received a card from her daughter and son-in-law from a captive cove in the Caribbean, which was all very congenial, except that she only had three sons.

At first there was babble and bedlam in the boroughs. People were baffled and bewildered. They soon found out, because they were very nosy, that Milford was a bit dyslexic. He inaccurately interchanged house numbers, so that for him the number 69 looked like number 96. A common mistake! More than likely, because of his dyslexia, in school he had subsisted at the southern extremity of standard assessments. But as he always maintained so eloquently, "I can only do so much. I am only one male man."

Masses of people were now all marching about with the mission of trying to find the owners of the mistaken and misplaced mail. They met many neighbours they hadn't monitored in years. They extended extensive invitations to friends and family members whom they had deemed ineligible in innumerable instances before.

"This is horrible," they said, but didn't really mean it. "Milford is the worst mailperson we have ever had." This was true. All the people, including visitors, had visions of protesting publicly on the park podium, of all the civilians climbing up and standing on this petite platform, looking down on a sole and solitary figure in the park, and that was Milford.

But before they could actually say those four frightening words which are: "Milford, you are fired," they pondered.

People soon came to the realization and mumbled that their murky and mundane, melancholy lives had actually been turned around. None of the townspeople had been moved to move this much in many a moon. They were now fit and fulfilled. They were now getting out of their musty and mouldy dwelling and getting much more fresh air. They were meeting and greeting and inviting people they had not seen in many years.

They did the only thing that was deemed mandatory. Milford received a large pay raise and continued to be the town's mailman **and they all ...**

East Gwillimbury

Porter the Pipefitter

There is a town called East Gwillimbury. It is situated south-east of North Gwillimbury, north-east of South Gwillimbury and directly east of West Gwillimbury.

Economic times had been hard, so the town council decided to build some subsidized housing for those who could otherwise not afford to buy a place of their own. However, most of the land which had been designated for development had been developed. And so the town council had the brilliant idea of putting up the housing a bit out of town, close to the presently closed quarry. It should be noted here that all the Gwillimbury towns, East, West, North and South could have been one large metropolis, were it not for the huge quarry that was smack dab in the middle of all the towns. It was an eyesore and blight, so most people kept away from it.

Construction began on the massive townhouse complex and bulldozers dozed for many weeks. Water mains had to be brought in. The city crew began their monstrous undertaking to bring these very large pipes to the gigantic construction site.

After quite some time, the rough construction phase was finally finished. Walls had been erected, electrical wires had been strung, and pipes had been installed in all the buildings. Now the giant multiplex needed to be hooked up to the water main. The pipes within the buildings were put under pressure in order for them to be monitored for leaks. There didn't seem to be any.

Porter, an apprentice pipefitter, had recently been hired by the City of East Gwillimbury. He was a very personable person, dedicated worker, and his supervisors were very impressed. "Porter, please pay attention," said his supervisor one day. "These pipes will be bringing precious water to the people of *Panorama Point*," the name of the townhouse complex.

"Stay and monitor the pipes to see that all is well," said his supervisor one Friday afternoon. "Because it is a long weekend and we have Monday off, I am going fishing with my buddies and I still need to get ready. Keep your eye on this water main and if anything happens, you know how to turn the water off."

Porter, who wanted to make some brownie points with his supervisor, agreed to stay late; so Friday afternoon he was the sole and solitary person who remained at the site. He, however, had other things on his mind. He had met a very beautiful young lady from West Gwillimbury at a dance a week ago and had made arrangements to pick her up at 6:00 p.m. and take her to South Gwillimbury to a bar where a new band was making its debut. This date was actually all he had on his mind. He forgot all about the water main, he forgot about the pressure in the pipes and he didn't worry about any potential leaks. He left at 3:55 p.m., a bit too early before the proper testing had been completed.

As you might imagine, with no one at the site to monitor it, the water main burst at precisely 3:59 p.m. on Friday afternoon. Well, the construction site was so far out of town nobody noticed.

The water kept bubbling and spurting, surging and gushing and pouring out of the main. First there was a trickle, then a stream and soon a mini Niagara Falls because all of the water rushed over the brink and down the steep quarry walls into the pit.

And when was this noticed? Tuesday morning at 6:55 a.m., when the first construction workers showed up at the site. Horror, disbelief, astonishment, bewilderment, bafflement, befuddlement and near panic! "What should we do?" they cried. "Someone turn off the water," was heard. "Who was the idiot who allowed this to happen," was another comment.

Porter and his supervisor showed up at 7:00 a.m. and knew right away whose fault this mess had been. Porter was ready for a tongue lashing, a shouting spree, a plethora of verbal abuse, his pink slip, but things don't always happen the way one might expect. Within a few minutes the news media were there: J.J. from the *South Gwillimbury Gazette* and D.J. from the West Gwillimbury radio station, *WGRD*. The mayor and the councilors soon arrived and there was such mayhem and confusion that one didn't know what to expect next.

The townspeople, who by now had all returned from their cottages, had received text messages from their friends and neighbours, and had come to the construction site to gawk.

All the Gwillimates looked down into the quarry, which was now one-third filled with water, and they looked at each other. The mayor, being a natural born leader, made an announcement. When asked by his councilors as to what should be done, he replied, "We will let the water run until the quarry is full," he said. "Then we will have a beautiful lake."

After the mayor's grandiose announcement, the townspeople looked at one another, they looked at the mayor and his councilors. They were speechless when asked to make a statement for the *South Gwillimbury Gazette* or make a comment to the West Gwillimbury Radio reporter from *WGRD*.

And so the ugly hole in the middle of all four communities, the old quarry, soon became a beautiful lake. Before long the townspeople built a walking, running and biking path all around the lake. Trees, shrubs and flowers were planted, grass was laid and in a little while the park became the envy of many communities within the vicinity.

And what happened to Porter? Well, he received the keys to all the towns of Gwillimbury: North, South, East and West. How could they now fire him? Impossible! Like they say in both industry and the government, if you want a promotion you have to do a really terrible job. Since Porter certainly had done a horrible job he qualified for a promotion. He became the marketing director of all four towns and did a much better job than he did as a pipefitter.

As an amateur scuba diver, Porter made good use of his knowledge. Diving clubs were invited to dive in the quarry lake to look at all the discarded cars, bulldozers and other heavy machinery which had been left at the bottom.

Other objects were found at the bottom of the quarry, such as an old barge and a chest, which was rumoured to be filled with treasure. Large fish could be seen ogling the scuba gogglers. How they had grown so quickly was a mystery to all except those who had brought them there from the lakes by their cottages. Everyone worked hard to make this lake a beautiful place for all the Gwillimates and their visitors. Before long you could see people walking, jogging, biking, swimming, and also canoeing, and sailing on the lake.

And the residents, who at first had been quite despondent over having to live in a housing complex near an abandoned quarry, now owned prime real estate on the shore of Lake Gwillimbury.

And so all the Gwillimates, South, West, North and East lived happily ever after.

HEIDI KLOSE lives in the Niagara Region, 165 kilometres south-east of West Gwillimbury. *Gwillimbury Tales* is her eighth children's book, following *The French River Delta: The Legend of Makadewaa*, *A French River Adventure*, *Piglets on the Wing*, *Piglets to the Rescue* - transcribed into German as *Fliegende Schweinchen* and *Rettung der Schweinchen* , and *The Problem With…*, all available on Amazon.

www.ingramcontent.com/pod-product-compliance
Lightning Source LLC
Chambersburg PA
CBHW040859120626
46551CB00001B/92